KB266073

오늘이라는 선물

오늘이라는 선물

한소영 시집

문화앤피플

별이 되기 위한 질량

"가슴 뛰는 삶을 살아라." 젊은 날, 책 속에서 읽었던 이 말의 뜻을 이제야 좀 알 것 같습니다. 그것은 단순히 청춘의 뜨거운 열정만을 뜻하는 것이 아니었습니다. 20대와 30대의 가슴 뜀이 세상을 향해 맹목적으로 질주하는 '팽창의 에너지'였다면, 오십이 넘어 느끼는 지금의 가슴 뜀은 내 안의 밀도가 꽉 차올라 비로소 빚어내는 '묵직한 공명'인 것같습니다. 아직 채워지지 않았던 지난날의 나는 이 말의 무게를 몰랐습니다. 우주의 먼지들이 모여 엄청난 압력을 견뎌야 스스로 빛을 내는 별(恒星)이 되듯, 우리 삶 또한 '별의 재료'가 충분히 쌓여야 비로소 빛을 낼 수 있는 때가

오기 때문입니다. 이제야 나는 진정으로 가슴이 뜁니다. 내게 주어졌던 그 참 마음 고생 많았던 서툰 시절들 그것은 내 안의 별이 빛나기 위해 반드시 필요했던 '질량'이었습니다. 그 무거운 질량이 임계점에 다다라서야 비로소 삶은 빛을 낼 준비를 합니다.

아버지 감사합니다. 지나온 모든 것이 별이 되기 위한 과정이었음을 이제는 압니다. 나에게 허락된 이 질량과 빛을 향해 나아가는 이 길에 깊이 감사합니다.

2026년 3월에

한 소 영

The Mass Required to Become a Star

Live a life that makes your heart race.

I read these words in a book long ago, in my youth.

Only now do I begin to grasp what they truly meant.

It was never simply about the burning passion of youth.

If the racing heart of my twenties and thirties was an energy of expansion – charging blindly toward the world – then the racing heart I feel now, past fifty, is something different. It is a deep resonance, born only when the density within has finally grown full.

In those unfulfilled days, I did not know the gravity of such words.

Just as cosmic dust must gather and endure immense pressure before it can become a star that shines by its own light, our lives, too, must accumulate enough stellar matter before the time comes to emit light.

Only *now* does my heart truly race.

All those clumsy years given to me - so full of inner turmoil - they were the massmy star required to shine. Only when that heavy mass reaches its critical point does a life become ready to give off light.

Father, I thank you.

I know now that everything I have lived through was part of becoming a star. For this mass I have been granted, and for this path toward light, I am deeply grateful.

In March 2026
Han So - young

별이 되기 위한 질량
The Mass Required to Become a Star

04

Part 1. 공 명   *Resonance*

-내 마음의 울림이 당신에게 닿을 때
When the trembling of my heart reaches yours

우주의 공식
The Equation of the Universe — 14

질량에 대하여
On Mass — 18

E=mc²
E=mc² — 22

무리수를 덮은 사람들
Those Who Drowned the Irrational — 26

자기장
Magnetic Field — 30

자석
Magnet — 32

창조의 원리
The Principle of Creation — 34

내가 눈을 뜨자, 우주가 비로소 존재했다
A Sliver of Difference — 36

닮음
Resemblance — 40

남 탓이라는 독
The Poiason Called Blame — 44

이해라는 빛
The Light Called Understanding — 48

꽃의 기도
The Flower's Prayer — 52

고요, 그 이전(혹은 숫자 0)
Stillness, Before That (or, the Number Zero) — 56

Part 2. 인 연   *Affinity*

-길 위에서 만난 소중한 선물
A Precious Gift Found on the Path of Living

탁발 *Alms*	62
인연이라는 숲 *The Forest Called Affinity*	66
나의 변주곡 *Variations on My Life*	72
아픔 *Pain*	80
영혼 없는 거래 *A Transaction Without Soul*	84
쥔 손과 빈 손 *The Clenched Hand and the Open Palm*	86
고풀이 *Untying the Knot*	88
닿지 않는 말 *Words Against Walls*	92
네모난 창 *The Square Window*	96
하루 *Just Another Day*	100
신을 닮아가는 여정 *The Journey of Becoming Round*	104
파문 *Ripple*	108
유연함 *Flexibility*	110
껍질 *Peel*	114

Part 3. 창 조 *Creation*

- 함께 어울려 빚어내는 빛
The Light We Shape Together

하늘 천(天) *Heaven (天)*	118
땅 지(地) *Earth (地)*	120
사람 인(人) *Humanity (人)*	122
흔적 *Trace*	124
별 *Star*	126
걸음의 이치 *The Principle of Walking- Heaven, Human, Earth*	128
구덩이 *Pit*	132
선택 *Choice*	136
빈칸 *Blank Space*	138
고요한 자리 *The Still Place*	142
자국으로 흐르다 *Flowing as Traces*	146
호흡 *Breath*	150
■ 천(天) 지(地) 인(人) 그림설명 하늘 천(天) 땅 지(地) 사람 인(人) *Heaven (天) Earth (地) Humanity (人)*	154

The tears I swallowed alone through all those silent years have become, at last, a song—deep and low. My heart begins to tremble, small vibrations at first. May this quivering ride the wind across the distance, and brush, ever so gently, the edges of your heart.

내 마음의 울림이 당신에게 닿을 때

When the trembling of my heart reaches yours

오랜 시간 홀로 삼켰던 눈물들이 이제는 깊고 낮은 노래가 되었습니다. 내 마음이 먼저 작게 떨리기 시작합니다. 이 떨림이 바람을 타고 넘어가당신의 마음 가장자리라도 살며시 건드릴 수 있기를.

우주의 공식

태초에 빛이 있었습니다

빛은 달리기를 멈추고
몸을 웅크렸습니다

그렇게
흙이 되고
바다가 되고
마침내 당신이 되었습니다

당신의 몸은
빛의 속도로 묶어둔
잠든 별빛입니다

우리가 살아간다는 것은
그 매듭을 푸는 일입니다

땀 흘려 일하고
가슴 태워 사랑하고
생을 바쳐 무언가를 지켜내는 일

갇혀 있던 빛이
다시 하늘로 돌아가는 것입니다

빛이 멈추어 당신이 되었고
당신이 타올라
사랑이 되었습니다

The Equation of the Universe

In the beginning, there was light.

Light grew so lonely.

It stopped running

and curled into itself.

And so energy

became matter.

It became soil,

became sea,

and at last, became you.

Your body is

sleeping starlight,

bound at the speed of light.

To live

is to untie that knot.

To labor until we sweat,

to love until our hearts burn,

to give our lives protecting something.

This is the sacred offering –

releasing the light once held captive

back into the sky.

Light paused and became you.

You blazed and became love.

This is the covenant by which the world was made,

the unchanging law of the universe.

질량에 대하여

나의 무게를
저울 위 숫자로 재지 마십시오

내가 말하는 무게는
삼켜온 눈물의 농도이고
무너지며 쌓아 올린 인내의 두께입니다

깊은 바닥을 친 사람의 삶은
그만큼 단단합니다

이 묵직한 삶이
빛처럼 빠른 깨달음을 만날 때
시련은 지혜가 되고
상처는 사랑이 됩니다

가벼운 삶은
결코 낼 수 없는 빛

나는 이제
내 삶의 무게를 사랑합니다
그것이 나를 밝게 태울
유일한 연료임을 알기에

On Mass

Do not measure my weight
by the number on a scale.

The weight I speak of
is the density of swallowed tears,
the thickness of patience
built up through collapse.

A life that has struck rock bottom –
that life is solid.

When this heavy existence
meets an insight swift as light,
trials become wisdom,
wounds become love.

A life lived lightly

can never emit such radiance.

I have come to love

the weight of my life –

knowing it is the only fuel

that will burn me bright.

E=mc²

E=mc².
그건 등식이 아니라 문이었다

보이지 않는 것이
만져지는 것으로 건너오는
문이었다

그 문이 열리자
시간이 흐르고
공간이 펼쳐졌다

떠돌던 에너지들이
서로를 끌어안아
별이 되고
흙이 되고
우리가 되었다

우연히 흩뿌려진 것이 아니다
태초의 무엇이
자신을 걸고 통과한 것이다

138억 년 전 열린 그 문이
지금 내 안에서
여전히 열려 있다

E=mc²

E=mc².
It was not an equation—
it was a door.

A door through which
the invisible
crossed over into touch.

When that door opened,
time began to flow,
space unfurled.

Wandering energies
embraced one another,
becoming stars,
becoming soil,
becoming us.

This was no accident of scattering.
Something ancient wagered itself
and crossed over.

The door that opened 13.8 billion years ago
remains open still –
here, inside me.

무리수를 덮은 사람들

피타고라스는 믿고 싶었다
세상의 모든 것이
1, 2, 3...
그 단단한 질서 안에 모든 것이 담기기를

그러나
끝도 없이 이어지는 숫자가 튀어나왔을 때
그들은 두려움에 떨며
발견자의 입을 막고
바다에 던졌다

수천 년이 지난 지금
우리는 무엇이 달라졌는가

보이는 아파트 평수는 믿으면서
보이지 않는 평안은 믿지 않는다

통장에 찍힌 숫자는 맹신하면서

가슴에 찍힌 상처는 외면한다

딱 떨어지지 않으면 불안해하고
손에 잡히지 않으면 없다고 말한다

그러나 보라
정사각형의 반듯한 변이 아니라
그 사이를 가로지르는 대각선이
도형을 지탱하고 있음을

우리의 삶을 진짜로 지탱하는 것은
계산기로 두드릴 수 없는 사랑
측정되지 않는 슬픔
나누어 떨어지지 않는 그리움이다

우리는 여전히
손에 든 낡은 자 하나로
무한한 우주를 잴 수 있다 믿는
어리석은 피타고라스의 제자들이다

Those Who Drowned the Irrational

Pythagoras wanted to believe
that everything in the world
could be held within
1, 2, 3...
that solid order.

But when a number emerged
that stretched on without end,
they trembled with fear,
silenced the one who found it,
and cast him into the sea.

Thousands of years have passed.
What has changed?

We believe in the square footage of apartments
but not in invisible peace.
We place blind faith in bank account digits

but look away from wounds etched in the heart.

If it doesn't divide evenly, we grow anxious.
If we cannot hold it, we say it does not exist.

But look it is not the square's tidy edges
but the diagonal cutting through
that holds the shape together.

What truly sustains our lives
is love no calculator can tally,
grief no instrument can measure,
longing that will not divide into whole numbers.

We remain, still,
foolish disciples of Pythagoras –
believing we can measure
an infinite universe
with the worn ruler in our hands.

자기장

가르치지 않아도 배웁니다

자석 곁의 쇠붙이가
저도 모르게 자성을 띠듯

아이는 나의 공기를
숨 쉬듯 마시며 자랍니다

내가 떨면 아이도 떨고
내가 고요하면 아이도 고요합니다

나의 기쁨도 슬픔도
감추고 싶던 그림자까지
보이지 않는 선을 타고 흘러가

아이는 어느새
나를 닮은 작은 자석이 되어 있었습니다

Magnetic Field

They learn without being taught.

Like iron near a magnet
taking on its charge unaware,

a child breathes in my atmosphere,
inhaling it like air.

When I tremble, the child trembles.
When I am still, the child is still.

My joy, my sorrow,
even the shadows I tried to hide –
all flow along invisible lines.

Before I knew it,
the child had become
a small magnet
shaped like me.

자석

밀어낸 것은 단호함이 아니라
상처받기 싫은 두려움이었다

붙잡은 것은 애틋함이 아니라
혼자이기 싫은 외로움이었다

밀어내면 외로웠고
붙잡으면 두려웠으니

도망치고 싶은 마음과
머물고 싶은 마음은
결국 한 몸이었다

몸을 깨뜨려 조각을 내어도
어김없이 등을 맞대고 다시 돋아나는

그 모순이
나라는 사람이다

Magnet

What pushed away was not resolve –
it was fear of being hurt.

What held on was not tenderness –
it was loneliness, dreading solitude.

Pushing away, I was lonely.
Holding on, I was afraid.

The urge to flee
and the longing to stay
were, in the end, one body.

Even if I shatter myself into pieces,
without fail, they grow back –
poles pressed together, back to back.

That contradiction
is the person I am.

창조의 원리

허공은 비어있지 않다
무엇이든 될 수 있는
가능성으로 가득하다

그 바다에
내가 생각이라는 파동을 보내고
말이라는 진동을 더하는 순간

흐르던 것이 굳어져
현실이 된다

벽이 되기도 하고
문이 되기도 한다

내가 사는 세상은
허공의 가능성을
내가 얼려 만든 것이다

The Principle of Creation

The void is not empty.
It brims with possibility –
anything it might become.

Into that sea
I send a ripple called thought,
add a vibration called word.

In that moment,
what was flowing
solidifies
and becomes real.

Sometimes a wall.
Sometimes a door.

The world I live in
is what I have frozen
from the void's infinite possibility.

내가 눈을 뜨자, 우주가 비로소 존재했다

1

아직 아무것도 아니다

희뿌연 숨결들이 허공에 떠돈다
비명인지 노래인지 알 수 없는 떨림들

부딪히지 않았으므로 소리가 없고
담지 않았으므로 모양이 없다

바다인가 사막인가
내가 눈뜨기 전
세상은 캄캄한 진동일 뿐

2

내가 '사랑'이라 읊조리자
안개가 붉은 꽃잎을 터트렸다

내가 '상처'라 찡그리자
바람이 칼날이 되어 내 살을 베었다

내 시선이 닿는 순간
물렁하던 공기가 돌이 되어 떨어진다

3
이제야 알았다

내가 쏘아 올린 것이
거울에 반사되어 돌아왔을 뿐

내가 웃으면 세상이 웃고
내가 울면 세상이 운다

A Sliver of Difference

Noise is noise

not because the sound is loud,

but because my attention lingers there.

Music does not drown out noise.

It merely helps my heart

remember its original rhythm.

The moment I withdraw

that single thought called disturbance –

the grating voices become scenery,

the sharp worries, flowing water.

The world has never changed.

In that instant when I retune
the frequency within –

everything returns to its place.

닮음

1
아이는
부모의 등 뒤에서
세상을 읽는 법을 배운다

말보다 먼저
내 한숨이 멈추는 지점을
눈빛이 흔들리는 각도를
제 몸에 새긴다

물려준 적 없으나
아이는 이미 쥐고 있었다
나를 잠식했던 오래된 파동을

2
우리는 너무 닮아
서로를 지나치지 못한다

내 안의 가시와 네 안의 가시가 만날 때
파도는 잦아들지 않고
더 높이 솟는다

너를 보며 화가 난 건
네 뒤에 숨은 나를 들켰기 때문일까

3
나의 낡은 삶이
너의 궤도가 되지 않기를

부딪히며 깨닫는다

이 공명을 멈추려면
거울 속 너를 탓할 게 아니라
파동의 진원지
내 마음이 먼저
고요해져야 했다

Resemblance

I

A child learns to read the world
from following in the parents' footsteps.

Before words,
they etch into their body
the point where my sigh catches,
the angle at which my gaze wavers.

I never handed it down,
yet the child already held it –
the old frequency that once consumed me.

II

We are too alike
to simply pass each other by.

When the thorn in me
meets the thorn in you,

the waves do not settle –
they rise higher.

Was I angry at you
because I was caught –
glimpsing myself hiding behind you?
III
May my worn-out life
not become the orbit you follow.

Through collision, I learn:

to stop this resonance,
I must not blame the you inside the mirror.
The epicenter of the wave,
my own heart,
had to grow still first.

남 탓이라는 독

벗어나고 싶어
나는 소리를 질렀다

네가 문제라고
세상이 틀렸다고

그러나 내가 휘두른 것은
망치가 아니라
칼날을 거꾸로 쥔 칼이었다

세상은 거대한 거울
밖을 향해 쏜 화살은
모두 나에게 돌아온다

남을 탓하는 손가락질은
내 눈을 찌르는 흉기였고

세상을 향한 저주는
내일의 나에게 보내는
부고장이었다

나아지려 발버둥칠수록
더 빠르게 무너졌다

남을 탓하며 구원을 바라는 것은
독약을 마시며
병이 낫기를 기도하는 것

The Poison Called Blame

Desperate to break free,
I screamed!

You are the problem. The world is wrong.

But what I swung
was not a hammer –
it was a blade gripped by the wrong end.

The world is a vast mirror.
Every arrow shot outward
returns to the one who fired it.

The finger I pointed at others
was a weapon piercing my own eyes.

The curses I hurled at the world

were obituaries

addressed to my future self.

The harder I thrashed to improve,

the faster I crumbled.

To blame others while hoping for salvation

is to drink poison

and pray for healing.

이해라는 빛

어둠을 탓하며 휘두르던
칼날이 손에서 떨어졌다

불행의 진원지가
나의 흔들리는 마음이었음을
알아차린 순간

멈추지 않을 것 같던 떨림이
고요해졌다

내가 왜 그토록
칼을 휘둘렀는지
이제야 보인다

상처받지 않으려고
먼저 베려 했던 것

칼이 떨어진 자리에
빈 손이 남았다

그 빈 손으로
처음으로
나를 안았다

The Light Called Understanding

The blade I swung

cursing the darkness

fell from my hand.

The moment I saw

that the epicenter of my suffering

was my own trembling heart –

the shaking that seemed it would never stop

grew still.

Only now do I see

why I swung so desperately.

I tried to cut first

so I would not be cut.

Where the blade fell,
empty hands remained.

With those empty hands,
for the first time,
I held myself.

꽃의 기도

색을 다 가지려 했다면
너는 캄캄한 어둠이 되었을 것이다

욕심 없이
빛을 허공으로 밀어내었기에
비로소 붉고 푸른 얼굴을 얻었다

평화로워 보이는 저 몸짓도
사실은 치열한 생존의 춤이다

어둠에 잠기지 않으려
빛 오는 쪽으로 기어이 고개 트는
맹목의 의지

꽃이 빛을 보며 웃을 수 있는 건
빛을 보지 못한 등 뒤의 줄기가
가장 부지런히 자라나
제 몸을 휘어지게 만들었기 때문이다

향기는 말이 없고
색채는 소리가 없으나

피어 있는 그 존재 자체가
이미 거대한 경전이다

The Flower's Prayer

Had you tried to keep all colors,

you would have become utter darkness.

Because you pushed light into the empty air

without grasping,

you finally received your red and blue face.

That peaceful gesture –

it is, in truth, a fierce dance of survival.

The blind will

that twists its neck toward light

refusing to drown in darkness.

A flower can smile at the sun

because the stem behind it, unseen,

grew most diligently in shadow,
bending its own body.

Fragrance speaks no words.
Color makes no sound.

Yet the mere fact of blooming
is already a vast scripture.

고요, 그 이전(혹은 숫자 0)

세상이 입체라 믿으며
부피를 키우고 면을 넓히며 살았다

내 생각과 네 생각이 부딪혀
파도는 쉴 새 없이 요동쳤다

이제 그 거품을 걷어낸다
면이 선이 되고
선이 다시 점으로 돌아간다

소란이 멈춘 자리에
고요가 남는다고 말하지만

영zero의 자리는
침묵이 아니다

평온이라는 느낌조차 생겨나기 전
고요라는 이름조차 붙기 전
아무것도 없었던 텅 빔

그 완벽한 없음 속에
모든 것이 녹아 있다

Stillness, Before That (or, the Number Zero)

Believing the world was solid,
I lived expanding volume, widening surface.

My thoughts clashed with yours –
waves churned without rest.

Now I sweep away the foam.
Surface becomes line.
Line returns to point.

They say stillness remains
where commotion has ceased.

But the place of zero
is not silence.

Before the feeling called peace arises,
before the name stillness
is even attached –

the utter emptiness
where nothing was.

Within that perfect absence,
everything dissolves.

We walked along different paths, yet, as though guided by a quiet promise, we find ourselves meeting here. All the painful hills I have crossed were, in truth, deliberate and devoted steps I had to take to reach you today.

길 위에서 만난 소중한 선물
A Precious Gift Found on the Path of Living

서로 다른 길을 걷던 우리가 약속이라도 한 듯 한곳에서 마주칩니다. 내가 지나온 그 모든 아픈 고개들은 사실 오늘 당신을 만나기 위해 꼭 거쳐야 했던 정성어린 발걸음이었습니다.

탁발

내 힘으로 땅을 일구어
먹고 사는 줄 알았다

이제야 본다
내 삶은 빈 그릇 하나 들고
세상이라는 문 앞을 서성인
긴 탁발의 여정이었다

어떤 날은 칭찬이라는 쌀밥을
어떤 날은 시련이라는 쉰 보리를
어떤 날은 모욕이라는 돌멩이를
받았다

젊은 날엔 따졌다
왜 내 그릇엔 찬바람뿐이냐고

이제서야 안다
그 쉰 밥도
그 돌멩이도
나를 굶어 죽지 않게 한
양식이었음을

이제 달다 쓰다 하지 않고
받겠다

가난도 풍요도
환호도 비난도

모두 나를 완성하려고
우주가 담아준 공양이므로

Alms

I thought I tilled the earth by my own strength,
fed myself by my own hands.

Only now do I see:
my life was a long journey of alms –
an empty bowl in hand,
wandering before the doors of the world.

Some days I received the rice of praise.Some days,
the soured barley of hardship.Some days, stones of
humiliation.

In my youth, I complained:
why does my bowl hold only cold wind?

Only now do I understand –

that soured grain,

those very stones,

were the sustenance

that kept me from starving.

Now I will receive

without calling it sweet or bitter.

Poverty and abundance,

cheers and scorn –

all of it, an offering

the universe placed in my bowl

to make me whole.

인연이라는 숲

1
부모는 땅이다

어둠 속에서
제 몸을 내어준 흙

그 대지가 있어
고개를 내밀었다

2
형제는 한 뿌리에서 돋아
다른 곳을 향해 뻗는 가지다

같은 바람에 흔들려
서로를 안다
비 오는 날이면
말없이 어깨를 부딪친다

3
남편은 맷돌이다

모난 돌을 깎아내려
요란하게 부딪쳤으나

그 끝에
우리는 둥글어지고 있었다

4
자식은 내 몸에 핀 꽃이다

나의 맑은 것과
탁한 것을 모두 비추는 거울

제 씨앗을 맺을 때까지
기꺼이 시들며 지켜볼
나의 다음 계절

5
이제 나는
홀로 선 나무다

네 계절이 나를 키웠고
이제는 나로 선다

받은 비와 햇살이
이만큼 자라게 했으니

이제는
지나는 이의 그늘이 되고
지친 새의 가지가 되어도 좋겠다

The Forest Called Affinity

I
My parents are earth.

The soil that gave its body
in the darkness.

Because that ground was there,
I pushed through and raised my head.

II
Siblings are branches
sprouting from one root,
reaching toward different skies.

Swayed by the same wind,
we know each other.
On rainy days,
we brush shoulders without a word.

III
A husband is a millstone.

To grind down the jagged edges,
we clashed, loud and rough.

Yet, by the end,
we were becoming round.

IV
A child is a flower blooming from my body.

A mirror reflecting
all that is clear in me,
and all that is murky.

Until they set their own seed,
I will gladly wither, watching over them –
my next season.

V
Now I am
a tree standing alone.

Four seasons raised me.
Now I stand as myself.

The rain and sunlight I received
have grown me this far.

So now,
let me be shade for those passing by,
a branch for the weary bird.

나의 변주곡

20대, 바람
어디서 불어와
어디로 가는지 몰랐다

잡히지 않는 것들을 쫓았고
흔들림조차 춤이라 믿고 싶었다

30대, 산
무거운 것들이 어깨를 눌렀다
아무도 없었다

그래도 일어섰다
나였을까
무엇이 나를 일으켜 세웠을까

40대, 점
그토록 타오르고 싶었다

지나온 모든 것을 모아
단 하나의 지금으로 터뜨리고 싶었다

뒤돌아보지 않으리라
내 모든 것을 던져서라도

그것은
찬란하게 타오르고자 했던
내 마음의 외침이었다

40대 후반, 꽃
이제는 미움 없이
사랑만으로 숨 쉬고 싶었다
나를 태운 열기가 식기 전에
그 온기로 꽃을 피웠다

눈물마저 거름이 되었다

50대, 수레바퀴

꽃이 지고 난 자리에

비로소 세상이 보인다

내가 울어도 웃어도

밤은 가고 아침이 온다

이제 나는

흐르는 것들을 그대로 껴안는다

[작가 노트]
20대 - 조용필의 바람의 노래
30대 - You raise me up
40대 - This is the moment
40대 후반 - 백만송이 장미
50대 - Ill Mondo

Variations on My Life

Twenties – Wind
I did not know
where I blew from,
where I was going.

I chased what could not be caught,
wanting to believe even my trembling was a dance.

Thirties – Mountain
Heavy things pressed down on my shoulders.
No one was there –
only the mountain, and my breath.

Still, I rose.
Was it me?
What was it that lifted me?

Forties - Point

How desperately I wanted to burn.

I wanted to gather everything I had lived through
and explode it into a single now.

I would not look back -
even if it meant throwing all of myself into it.

That was
the cry of my heart,
longing to blaze in splendor.

Late Forties - Flower

Now I wanted to breathe
only with love, without hatred.

Before the heat that burned me cooled,

I used its warmth to bloom.

Even my tears became compost.

Fifties – Cartwheel

Where the flower fell away,

the world finally comes into view.

Whether I weep or laugh,

night passes and morning comes.

Now I embrace

what flows, as it flows.

[Author's Note]

Twenties - "The Wind's Song" by Cho Yong-pil

Thirties - "You Raise Me Up"

Forties - "This Is the Moment"

Late forties - "A Million Roses"

Fifties - "Il Mondo"

영혼 없는 거래

돈으로 시간을 샀기에
주인은 사람을 부속품이라 여겼다

시간을 돈으로 바꿨기에
일꾼은 일을 감옥이라 여겼다

마음이 빠진 거래는 늘 차갑다

주인은 모른다
억지로 시킨 일 열 가지보다
스스로 한 일 한 가지가
더 크다는 것을

일꾼도 모른다
요령 피워 덜어낸 그 일이
주인의 몫이 아니라
내 성장을 덜어낸 것임을

서로 밑지지 않으려
눈을 부라리는 사이

일터는 전쟁터가 되고
우리는 서로에게
기계가 되어간다

사람의 온기는 어디 가고
계산기 소리만 울린다

A Transaction Without Soul

Because he bought time with money,

the owner saw people as parts.

Because she traded time for money,

the worker saw work as a prison.

A deal drained of heart is always cold.

The owner does not know

that one task done willingly

outweighs ten tasks forced.

The worker does not know

that the labor she skimped with clever shortcuts

was not taken from the owner's share,

but shaved from her own becoming.

Each refusing to lose ground,
glaring, watching –

the workplace becomes a battlefield,
and we become machines
to one another.

Where has human warmth gone?
Only the sound of calculators remains.

아픔

'견딜 수 없다'는 절규 앞에서
나는 고작
그 말이 '아프다'는 뜻인 줄만 알았다

껍데기만 이해하는 나를 보며
묻는다

이 좁은 눈으로
어찌 타인의 세상을 보려 하는가

Pain

Before the cry of *I cannot bear this*, I understood
only that those words meant 'it hurts'.

Watching myself grasp nothing but the shell,
I ask:

With eyes this narrow,
how can I hope to see another's world?

쥔 손과 빈 손

꽉 쥔 주먹은
내 힘으로 세상을 잡으려 함이고

활짝 편 빈 손은
세상이 내게로 와 안기게 됨이라

애써 잡으려 할 땐
손가락 사이로 빠져나가더니

가만히 펴고 기다리니
나비가 날아와 앉는다

함은 고단하고
됨은 머무나니.

The Clenched Hand and the Open Palm

A fist clenched tight –

that is trying to seize the world by my own

strength.

A palm spread open and empty – that is letting the

world come and rest in me.

When I strained to grasp,

it slipped through my fingers.

When I simply opened my hand and waited,

a butterfly came and alighted.

Doing is weary.

Becoming abides.

고풀이

누가 나를 묶었는가

가난이라는 밧줄로
책임이라는 사슬로
누가 나를 이 기둥에 묶었는가

평생을 물었다
세상을 향해 물었다

몇십 년을 돌고 돌아
이제 밧줄의 끝을 본다

아,
그 밧줄을 잡고 있던 것은
나였다

놓으면 큰일 난다 믿고
내 손으로 내 발목을 묶은 채
가지 못한다 울고 있었다

이제 손에 힘을 뺀다

툭,
밧줄이 떨어진다

나는 묶여 있던 것이 아니라
스스로를 가두고 있었다

고를 푼다는 것은
남을 용서하는 일이 아니라
버텨온 나를
놓아주는 일이었다

Untying the Knot

Who bound me?

With a rope called poverty,
with chains called duty –
who tied me to this post?

I asked all my life.
I asked the world.

After decades of circling,
I finally see where the rope ends.

Ah –
the one holding it
was me.

Believing disaster would come if I let go,
I bound my own ankles with my own hands,
weeping that I could not move.

Now I release the grip.

Thud! – the rope falls.

I was never bound.
I was imprisoning myself.

To untie the knot
was never about forgiving others.
It was about releasing
the self that had endured so long.

닿지 않는 말

같은 말을 쓰는데도
우리는 이방인 같다

나의 '힘듦'이
너의 귀에는 '투정'으로 들리고

너의 '위로'가
나의 가슴엔 '참견'으로 꽂힌다.

마주 보고 앉아 떠들지만
그것은 대화가 아니라
각자의 벽에 대고 외치는 독백

내 마음의 창틀이 좁아
네 진심이 들어올 틈이 없고

네 생각의 문이 좁아
내 진실이 들어갈 자리가 없다

우리는
가장 가까이 앉아서
가장 먼 곳을 헤맨다

Words Against Walls

We use the same words,

yet we remain strangers.

My *struggling* sounds like *whining* to your ears.

Your *comfort* lodges in my chest as *meddling*.

We sit face to face, talking,

yet it is not conversation –

just monologues shouted at our separate walls.

The window of my heart is too narrow

for your sincerity to enter.

The door of your mind is too narrow

for my truth to find a place.

We sit closest to each other,

wandering the farthest apart.

네모난 창

세상은 둥글기도 하고
모나기도 하고
때론 흐물거려 모양이 없는데

나는 네모난 창틀을 만들어
그 너머를 본다

창틀보다 큰 것은 잘려 나가고
창틀보다 작은 것은 초라해 보인다

내 창에 들어오지 않는 것은
틀렸다고 말한다

세상이 좁은 게 아닌데
내가 만든 창이 좁아 숨이 막힌다

아름다운 것들이
내 틀에 깎여 나가는 줄도 모르고

나는 오늘도
그 좁은 사각형만 세상의 전부라 믿으며
시비를 가른다

언제쯤
이 창을 깨트리고
문 밖으로 걸어 나가

그어진 세상이 아닌
날 것 그대로의 바람을 맞을까

The Square Window

The world is sometimes round,

sometimes angular,

sometimes shapeless and soft –

yet I have built a square frame

and look at the world through it.

What is larger than the frame gets cut away.

What is smaller looks pitiful.

What does not fit my window,

I call wrong.

The world is not narrow –

it is the window I made that suffocates me.

Not knowing that beautiful things
are being shaved away by my frame,

I go on today
believing that small square is the whole of the
world,
judging right from wrong.

When will I
shatter this window,
leave the lines behind,

and meet the wind as it is –
not a world drawn by lines,
but raw and whole.

하루

온전히 산다는 것은
고요함만을 찾는 일이 아니다

귓가에 닿는 소음
바람에 실려오는 냄새
사람들의 인기척

다정한 말소리만 있으면 좋으련만
때로는 날 선 욕소리가 날아와
마음 한구석을 찌른다

온전히 산다는 건
그 소란도
그로 인해 일렁이는 내 안의 울컥함도
외면하지 않고 마주하는 일

좋은 것만 골라내는 편식이 아니라

세상이 던지는 모든 소리를

나의 하루라는 그릇에

받아들이는 것

그것이 비로소

오늘을 사는 일

Just Another Day

To live fully

is not only to seek stillness.

The noise brushing my ears,

the scent carried on the wind,

the presence of people nearby.

I wish there were only tender words,

yet sometimes a sharp curse flies in

and pierces a corner of my heart.

To live fully

is to face that commotion –

and the surge rising within me because of it –

without turning away.

Not the picky eating that selects only what is
pleasant, but receiving every sound the world
throws into the bowl called my day.

That, at last,
is what it means to live today.

신을 닮아가는 여정

신은 완벽한 원.

모난 곳이 없어
누구를 찌르지도
어디에 걸리지도 않는다

사람은 모나다

내 고집이 너를 찌르고
내 욕심이 세상에 걸린다

그래서 신은
환경이라는 사포를 주었나 보다

사람에게 치여 깎이고
실패에 부딪혀 깨진다

아프다 비명 지르지만
사실은 나를 갈아내는 시간

이리 굴러 저리 부딪히며
날 선 모서리가 닳아 없어질 때마다
조금씩 부드러워진다

나를 둥글게 만드는 환경이
처음엔 형벌인 줄 알았으나
지나고 보니 은총이었다

오늘 또 한 번 깎이며
조금 더 둥근 나를 만난다

The Journey of Becoming Round

God is a perfect circle.

With no edges,
God pierces no one,
catches on nothing.

A person is angular.

My stubbornness pierces you.
My greed snags on the world.

So perhaps God gave us
an environment called sandpaper.

Worn down by people,
broken against failure.

I cry out in pain,

yet in truth, this is time grinding me smooth.

Rolling this way, colliding that way –

each time a sharp edge wears away,

I soften a little more.

The surroundings that round me –

I first thought them punishment.

Looking back, they were grace.

Today I am sanded once more,

and meet a slightly rounder self.

파문

고요한 호수 한가운데
물방울 하나가 떨어진다

작고 여린 시작이
나를 넘어 담장을 넘어
너의 기슭에 닿아
메마른 흙을 적신다

너와 내가
다른 뿌리가 아님을 알아
서로의 그늘이 되어주는 숲

내 안에서 시작된 작은 떨림이
천 리 밖 타인의 가슴까지 번져
봄바람처럼 데운다

그렇게 세상은
하나의 숨결로 평안해진다

Ripple

Into the stillness of a lake,
a single drop falls.

A small, tender beginning –
it moves beyond me, over the wall,
reaches your shore,
and moistens the parched soil.

Knowing we are not separate roots,
we become a forest
that offers each other shade.

The small trembling that began in me
warms the heart of a stranger a thousand miles
away.

When it spreads into the world
as a warm spring breeze,

the world, at last,
breathes as one and is at peace.

유연함

유연해지려 애쓰는 동안
몸은 외려 더 굳어졌다

부드러운 척하는 동안
속에서 금이 가고 있었다

나를 들여다보았을 때
비로소 네가 보였다

내 안의 구멍이 보일 때쯤
너도 환해졌다

나를 힘들게 한 사람
나를 기쁘게 한 일
그 모든 것이 스승이었다

내려놓았다
그것뿐이었는데

딱딱했던 것들이
스르르 풀렸다

그때 알았다
흐른다는 것이
무엇인지를

Flexibility

While I strained to become flexible,
my body only stiffened.

Pretending to be soft,
at some point
I snapped.

Flexibility
was never something forced into being.

When I looked at myself,
I began to see the other.

Why is this person
standing before me now?

By the time I could see
the holes within my deeper self,
the one before me became clear as well.

The person who exhausts me,
the work that delights me –

all of it, my lesson.

When I lowered myself and received,
what had been rigid
quietly loosened.

Water does not try to become.
It simply flows.

껍질

양파를 깐다

까고, 또 까고
눈물이 날 때까지 깠다

마침내 드러난
하얀 중심

열어보니
아무것도 없었다

아,
평생을 바쳐 하던 일이
이것이었구나

빈 손으로
웃음이 났다

Peel

I peel an onion.

Peel, and peel again –
I peel until tears come.

At last, the white center
is revealed.

I open it
and find nothing there.

Ah – so this is what I spent
my whole life doing.

With empty hands,
I laughed.

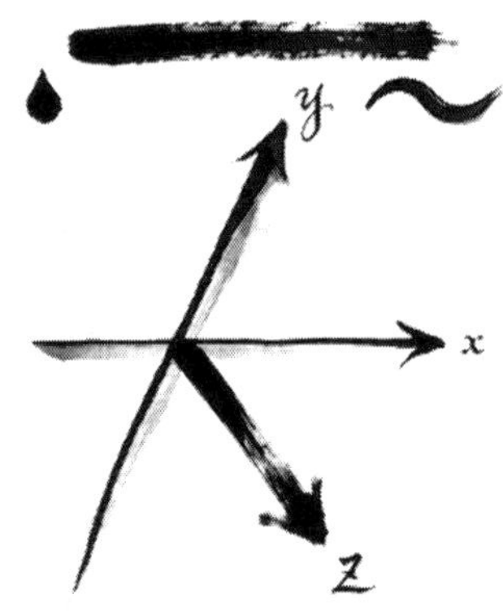

When two hearts meet and turn as one, the still world awakens into brightness.
To that far place I could never reach alone-now, borrowing each other's light, we set out to draw a new tomorrow together.

함께 어울려 빚어내는 빛
The Light We Shape Together

두 마음이 만나 같이 어울려 돌아갈 때, 멈춰 있던 세상은 비로소 환하게 깨어납니다. 혼자서는 결코 가볼 수 없던 저 먼 곳까지 이제는 서로의 빛을 빌려 새로운 내일을 함께 그려 나가려 합니다.

하늘 천(天)

본래 다 하늘이었기에
어디에도 하늘은 없었다

침묵하던 점 하나
스스로를 흔들어 선을 긋고
파동이 되어
무한의 잠을 깨웠다

그 떨림이 그려낸
세 번의 궤적은
어둠 속에
깊고 넓은 집을 지었다

무한 위에
태초의 선 하나 얹히자
우리는 고개 들어
그것을 하늘이라 불렀다

내 안의 작은 숨소리조차
멈추지 않고 달려온
그 점 하나의 노래였음을

Heaven, Sky, 天

Because all was sky from the beginning,
sky existed nowhere.

A single silent point
shook itself, drew a line,
became a wave,
and woke infinity from sleep.

The three paths traced by that trembling
built a house –
deep and wide –
within the darkness.

When that primordial line was laid
upon the infinite,
we lifted our heads and
called it sky.

Even the slightest breath within me –
it was the song of that single point,
running without pause.

사람 인(人)

영혼의 한 줄기 빛이 내려와도
혼자서는 대지에 발을 딛지 못해
기어이 또 하나의 숨결을 찾아간다

비스듬히 서로의 몸을 빌려
기대고 버티는 그 기울기

상대가 건네는 3
내가 세우는 7
그것이 맞물릴 때
비로소 사람으로 선다

한 획이 길어 상대를 짓누르거나
한 획이 짧아 허공에 겉돌지 않도록
3과 7의 결을 따라
묵묵히 제 자리를 지킨다

Being Human, 人

Even when a single ray of the soul descends,
it cannot plant its feet on earth alone –
so it seeks, inevitably, another breath.

Leaning at an angle, borrowing each other's bodies,
supporting and enduring in that tilt.

The three the other leans in,
the seven I stand firm –
only when they interlock
do we stand as human.

Neither stroke so long it crushes the other,
nor so short it drifts into empty air –
following the grain of three and seven,
each quietly holds its place.

땅 지(地)

하늘과 사람이
마음이라는 끈으로 묶여
비로소 이 대지 위에
발을 딛는다

단단하게 굳은 흙은
죽은 침묵이 아니라
태초의 뜨거운 파동이
질량의 옷을 입고 잠시 머무는 곳

뱀처럼 휘어지는 삶의 굴곡은
우리가 살아있다는
가장 정직한 신호

그 흔들림의 결을 따라
하늘의 뜻은 이 땅에
실체가 되어 흐른다

Earth, Ground, 地

Heaven and human,
bound by the thread called heart –
only then do we plant our feet
upon this ground.

Hardened soil
is not dead silence,
but a place where the primordial hot wave
rests a while, clothed in mass.

The serpentine curves of life
are the most honest signal
that we are alive.

Following the grain of that trembling,
the will of heaven flows into this earth,
becoming substance.

흔적

생각 하나가 일어났다

시간이 흐르자
생각은 계속 돌아왔다

외부와 부딪혀 파동이 일고
파동이 접혀 형태가 생겼다

이윽고 몸 어딘가에 자리 잡아
작은 신호를 보낸다

나 여기 있다고.

수많은 생각들 속에
신호는 묻힌다

Trace

A thought arose.

As time passed,
the thought kept returning.

It collided with the outside, waves formed.
The waves folded, taking shape.

In time, it settled somewhere in my body
and began to send a small signal.

I am here.

Among countless thoughts,
the signal was buried.

별

나는 한때 차가운 행성이었다
누가 빛을 비춰주지 않으면 그늘에 숨었고
힘든 일이 오면 밀어냈다

그땐 몰랐다

이제는 그냥 삼킨다.
미움도 서러움도 외로움도.

그러다 문득 빛이 난다

빛을 기다리던 행성이 스스로 빛나는 별이 되는 건
그렇게 시작된다

Star

I was once a cold planet.

Without someone to shine light on me, I hid in
shadow.

When hardship came, I pushed it away.

I did not know then.

Now, I simply swallow.

Hatred, sorrow, loneliness : all of it.

And suddenly, I glow.

This is how it begins –

the planet that waited for light

becoming a star that shines on its own.

걸음의 이치 - 천인지

걷는다는 것은
흐트러진 내 안을
다시 쌓아 올리는 일

골반이 땅이 되어
좌골의 뿌리를 깊이 내리면
흔들리던 대지가
비로소 고요해진다

땅이 든든해지자
척추라는 기둥이
스스로 솟아오른다

누가 시키지 않아도
가슴은 열리고
등에는 저절로 힘이 깃든다

땅이 나를
밀어 올리는 것이다

그때 머리는
짐을 내려놓고
하늘처럼 가벼워진다

긴장은 사라지고
맑은 공기만이 머문다

아래는 주춧돌이 되고
가운데는 기둥을 세우고
위는 하늘을 연다.

한 걸음 한 걸음이
무너진 우주를 다시 세우는
거룩한 제사였다

천인지(天人地)
하늘과 사람과 땅이
내 안에서 다시 만난다

The Principle of Walking- Heaven, Human, Earth

To walk
is to rebuild
what has scattered within.

When the pelvis becomes earth
and the sitting bones send roots deep down,
the trembling ground
finally grows still.

Once the earth is firm,
the spine - that pillar -
rises of its own accord.

Without being told,
the chest opens,
the back fills with strength.

The earth
is pushing me upward.

Then the head
sets down its burden
and becomes light as sky.

Tension vanishes.
Only clear air remains.

Below becomes foundation.
The center raises a pillar.
Above opens into sky.

Each step
was a sacred rite –
rebuilding a collapsed universe.

天人地 –
Heaven, Human, Earth –
meet again within me.

구덩이

1
길마다 구덩이가 패인 것이 아니다

두려움이 출렁일 때마다
세상이 가장 아픈 모양으로
굳었을 뿐

저 수렁은
누가 판 것이 아니라
내 불안이 만든 틀이었다

2
어쩐지 낯익은 어둠이라 했다

새 길을 가려 해도
자꾸 같은 낭떠러지 앞에 서는 건
주머니 속에
낡은 지도가 있기 때문이다

그 안의 한숨을
나침반 삼아 걸었기에
열심히 달려도
어디선가 본 막다른 길이었다

3
빠져나오려 소리칠수록
구덩이는 깊어진다

내 비명과
세상의 메아리가 닮아있어서

벗어나려는 몸부림이
오히려 벽을 두껍게 했다

구덩이를 메우는 건
몸부림이 아니라 멈춤

내 마음이 고요해질 때
단단했던 것이
다시 흐르기 시작한다

Pit

I
It is not that every road has a pit.

Each time fear surged,
the world hardened
into its most painful shape.

That mire –
no one dug it.
It was a mold my anxiety made.

II
No wonder the darkness felt familiar.

Even when I try a new road,
I keep standing before the same cliff –
because in my pocket
lies an old map.

Walking with its sighs
as my compass,

no matter how hard I ran,
I reached a dead end I had seen before.

III
The more I scream to escape,
the deeper the pit becomes.

My cries
and the world's echo
sound the same.

The struggle to break free
only thickened the walls.

What fills the pit
is not thrashing, but stillness.

When my heart grows quiet,
what had hardened
begins to flow again.

선택

내 안에 수만 가지 내가 있었다
그중 하나가
여기 서 있다

다른 우주가 아니라
내 안에 그들이 있다
태어나지 않은 채로

내가 이 하나를 꺼냈다
그래서 이것이
나의 진짜 삶이다

Choice

Ten thousand selves lived within me.

One of them

stands here now.

They are not in other universes –

they are inside me,

unborn.

I drew this one out.

And so this

is my true life.

빈칸

"안다"고 말하는 순간
세상은 입을 다문다

수천 년 동안
사과는 땅으로 떨어졌다
"당연하지"라며 지나친 사람들에게
하늘은 아무것도 보여주지 않았다

오직 "왜?"라고 물은 한 사람에게만
사과는 우주로 떨어졌다

"인생은 원래 고해야"
그렇게 덮어버린 사람은
평생 파도에 휩쓸린다

하지만 그 고통을 가만히 들여다본 사람은
알게 된다
이것이 나를 무너뜨리러 온 것이 아니라
나를 빚으러 온 불이었음을

안다는 마침표를 찍지 마라

마음에 빈칸을 남겨두는 사람에게만
숨겨진 것들이
별빛처럼 쏟아진다

Blank Space

The moment you say "I know,"
the world closes its mouth.

For thousands of years,
apples fell to the ground.
To those who passed by saying "obviously" -
the sky revealed nothing.

Only to the one who asked "Why?"
did the apple fall into the universe.

"Life is suffering, that's just how it is" -
those who cover it up this way
are tossed by waves their whole lives.

But those who gaze quietly into that pain

come to see:

this did not come to destroy me –

it was fire which come to shape me.

Do not place a period after knowing.

Only to those who leave a blank space in their
hearts
do hidden things
pour down like starlight.

고요한 자리

날아오는 것들을
밀어내는 대신
안으로 돌려본다

도망치던 발이
멈춘다

시끄러운 것은 늘 껍데기뿐
가장 뜨거운 불꽃은 소리가 없다

새어나가지 않고
고요히 삭인 것들이
언젠가 빛이 된다

세상이 회오리쳐도
가만히 서 있는다

태풍의 눈은
늘 고요하다

삼키고
견디고
지켜본다

그렇게 가만히 있으니
흔들리던 것들이
제자리를 찾아간다

The Still Place

Instead of pushing away
what flies toward me,
I turn inward.

The feet that fled
come to rest.

What is loud is always only the shell.
The hottest flame makes no sound.

What does not leak out,
what is quietly digested within –
one day becomes light.

Even when the world whirls,
I stand still.

The eye of the typhoon
is always calm.

Swallow.
Endure.
Watch.

Standing still like this,
what had been shaking
finds its place again.

자국으로 흐르다

우리는 점을 찍으려 애썼으나
정작 필요한 것은
점이 머물다 간 마른 자리였다

살아있는 점은
욕심이 되어 파도를 일으키고
형태가 바뀔 때마다
우리를 흔들리게 하지만

나를 채우던 색이 빠져나간
그 투명한 자국은
비로소 너를 향해 열린 길이 된다

나라는 점이 지워진 자리에
너라는 파동이 스며들고
서로의 깊이가 닿을 때
연결은 소유가 아닌 공명이 된다

이제 점은 없다
오직 서로에게 남긴
자국들만 있을 뿐

Flowing as Traces

We labored to make our mark,

yet what we truly needed

was the dry space where the mark had stained then

faded

A living dot

becomes desire, stirring waves –

each time it shifts form,

it shakes us.

But the transparent trace

left when my color has drained away

becomes, at last, a path opened toward you.

Where the dot called I
have been erased,
the wave called you
seeps in.

When our depths touch,
connection becomes
not possession,
but resonance.

Now there are no dots –
only the traces
we have left in one another.

호흡

찰나의 틈을 벌리는 것은
날카로운 지성이 아니다

깊고 부드러운
한 번의 숨

천천히 들이마시고
천천히 내쉰다

요동치던 것들이
가라앉는다

숨이 깊어질수록
찰나는 길어지고

길어진 찰나 속에서
그것들이 문장이 된다

말이 투명해진다
단순해진다

Breath

What opens a crack in the moment
is not sharp intellect.

It is one breath:
deep and soft.

Inhale slowly.
Exhale slowly.

What was churning
settles.

The deeper the breath,
the longer the moment grows.

Within that lengthened instant,

things become sentences.

Words grow transparent.

Simple.

하늘 천(天):
1차원의 점에서 시작된 3차원의 진동

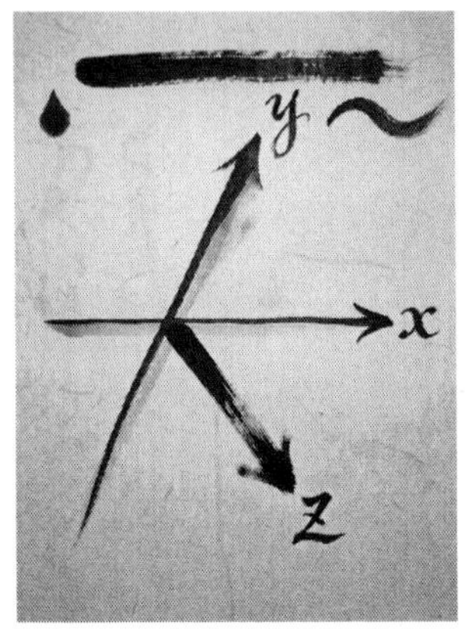

하늘을 뜻하는 '천(天)'의 맨 위, '한 일(一)'자를 90도 회전시키면 태초의 응축된 힘인 점(.)이 됩니다. 이 1차원의 점은 선이 되어 2차원으로 확장되고, 그 선이 요동치며 비로소 3차원의 파동을 형성합니다.

글자 하단의 '큰 대(大)'자는 단순한 형상이 아닙니다. 이는 입체 공간을 구성하는 x, y, z축을 형상화한 것으로, 하늘이란 곧 인간의 굴곡진 삶이 펼쳐지는 거대한 '3차원의 무대'임을 선언하고 있습니다. 즉, 하늘은 머리 위 먼 곳이 아니라, 무형의 에너지가 입체적인 현실로 구현되는 근원적 장(場)인 셈입니다.

Heaven (天):
A 3D Vibration Originating from a 1D Point

The top stroke of 'Heaven' (天), the character for 'one' (一), becomes the 'point (.)' – the primordial, condensed force – when rotated 90 degrees. This one-dimensional point expands into a line (2D), which then begins to oscillate, eventually forming a three-dimensional wave.

The lower part of the character, 'Big' (大), is more than just a shape; it represents the x, y, and z axesthat constitute physical space. It declares that Heaven is not a distant place above our heads, but a vast '3D stage'where the complexities of human life unfold. In short, Heaven is the fundamental field where formless energy is manifested into a tangible, three-dimensional reality.

땅 지(地):
파동의 시공간 위에 선 인간

'땅 지(地)'는 하늘의 기운과 인간이 마음(가슴)에서 결합하여 대지 위에 발을 붙인 형상입니다. 특히 뱀의 형상에서 유래한 '이끼야(也)'자에 주목해야 합니다. 뱀은 유연한 곡선을 그리며 나아가는 선형적 파동의 상징입니다.

결국 '지(地)'라는 글자는, 인간이 정지된 평면이 아니라 끊임없이 변화하고 출렁이는 3차원의 시공간속에서 생명력을 이어가고 있음을 정교하게 묘사하고 있습니다. 땅은 굳건한 바닥인 동시에, 하늘로부터 내려온 파동이 물질화되어 흐르는 역동적인 터전입니다.

Earth (地):
Humanity Standing Upon the Spacetime of Waves

The character for 'Earth' (地) illustrates the union of celestial energy and the human heart (chest), firmly rooted upon the ground. A key element here is the component '也', derived from the form of a snake. The snake serves as a symbol of a linear wave moving in flexible, rhythmic curves.

Thus, the character '地' elaborately depicts that humans do not exist on a static plane, but within a constantly shifting and undulating 3D spacetime. The Earth is both a solid foundation and a dynamic arena where the waves descending from Heaven materialize and flow.

사람 인(人):
우주의 황금률, 3:7의 법칙

마지막으로 '사람 인(人)'은 그 구조 자체로 우주의 균형점인 '3:7의 법칙'을 내포합니다. 두 선이 서로의 무게를 지탱하며 완벽한 각도를 이루는 모습은, 하늘의 이치와 땅의 생명력이 인간이라는 존재 안에서 어떻게 조화를 이루어야 하는지를 보여줍니다.

사람은 하늘의 파동을 받아 땅의 현실을 일궈내는 매개체이며, 그 존재 자체가 우주의 기하학적 완성이라 할 수 있습니다.

Humanity (人):
The Universal Golden Ratio, the 3:7 Law

Finally, the character for 'Human' (人) inherently embodies the '3:7 Law' – the equilibrium point of the universe. The way two lines lean against each other to support their collective weight at a perfect angle demonstrates how the principles of Heaven and the vitality of Earth should harmonize within a human being.

A human is the mediumthat receives the vibrations of Heaven to cultivate the reality of Earth; the very existence of humanity is the geometric completion of the universe.

오늘이라는 선물

초판인쇄 2026년 3월 30일
초판발행 2026년 3월 30일

지은이 한소영
펴낸이 이해경
편 집 박다연
펴낸곳 (주)문화앤피플뉴스
등록번호 제2024-000036호
주소 서울 중구 충무로2길 16, 4층 403호 (충무로4가, 동영빌딩)
대표전화 02)3295-3335
팩스 02)3295-3336
이메일 cnpnews@naver.com
홈페이지 www.cnpnews.co.kr

정가 13,000원
ISBN 979-11-94950-31-8(03810)